NATURAL WONDERS OF THE WORLD

CALIFORNIA'S REDWOOD FOREST

by Christy Mihaly

FOCUS READERS

FOCUS READERS

WWW.FOCUSREADERS.COM

Focus Readers is distributed by North Star Editions:
sales@northstareditions.com | 888-417-0195

Produced for Focus Readers by Red Line Editorial.

Content Consultant: Kevin O'Hara, PhD, Professor in the Department of Environmental Science, Policy, and Management at the University of California, Berkeley

Photographs ©: Hang Li/Shutterstock Images, cover, 1; noblige/iStockphoto, 4–5; CampPhoto/iStockphoto, 6, 22–23; Red Line Editorial, 9, 27; 4kodiak/iStockphoto, 10–11; StephanHoerold/iStockphoto, 13; Carol M. Highsmith/Highsmith Archive/Library of Congress, 15, 18, 29; Pawel Gaul/iStockphoto, 16–17; iacona/iStockphoto, 21; Pi-Lens/Shutterstock Images, 24–25

ISBN
978-1-63517-512-7 (hardcover)
978-1-63517-584-4 (paperback)
978-1-63517-728-2 (ebook pdf)
978-1-63517-656-8 (hosted ebook)

Library of Congress Control Number: 2017948117

Printed in the United States of America
Mankato, MN
November, 2017

ABOUT THE AUTHOR

Christy Mihaly first stood under the tall redwood trees, gazing upward, many years ago. She still remembers the wonder she felt then. Christy has studied environmental science, and she writes about nature, science, and history. She hopes this book will inspire future scientists, artists, and nature lovers.

TABLE OF CONTENTS

CHAPTER 1

THOSE AMAZING REDWOODS

California's wild and foggy north coast holds a natural wonder. It's the amazing redwood forest. This forest is home to the coast redwood trees. Coast redwoods are the world's tallest trees. They can grow higher than 30-story buildings. From the ground, a person cannot even see the treetops.

More than 500,000 people visited Redwood National Park in 2015.

The redwood forest begins on the coast of the Pacific Ocean and goes into nearby mountain ranges.

Coast redwoods are **evergreens**. They hold on to their needles all year long. This keeps the redwood forest dim and cool. Light shines softly through branches high above. Standing in this tall forest feels like being inside a huge church or temple.

Coast redwoods can live hundreds of years. Some are more than 2,000 years old. These same trees were alive when the ancient Romans ruled much of Europe and other nearby areas.

The redwoods are part of a rainy **ecosystem** called the **temperate rainforest**. Their natural range is in northern California and parts of Oregon.

THE WORLD'S TALLEST TREE

The world's tallest known living tree is a coast redwood. This tree is named Hyperion, after a mighty Greek god. Hyperion stands more than 379 feet (116 m) tall and is probably still growing. Adventurous scientists climbed to its top. They measured the tree by dropping a very long tape to the ground. Hyperion lives somewhere deep inside Redwood National Park. To protect this natural wonder, officials are keeping its exact location a secret.

Redwoods grow in an area that is 35 miles (56 km) wide and 450 miles (724 km) long. The redwoods can grow in regions that are up to 3,300 feet (1,006 m) above sea level. This puts them in the lower parts of the coastal mountain ranges.

Many kinds of plants grow in the redwood forests. Hundreds of animal **species** make their homes there, too. Birds nest in the trees. Banana slugs hide on the forest floor. Foxes hunt for mice among the shadows. Insects buzz. The giant trees are just one part of these amazing forests.

REDWOOD COMPARISONS

The tallest redwood trees tower over not only people, but other tall objects as well.

CHAPTER 2

FOREST OF LIVING FOSSILS

Scientists have found **fossils** of many kinds of redwoods. Some redwood fossils are 300 million years old. Most types of redwoods have gone extinct. But the coast redwood still exists. Today's coast redwoods look almost the same as those that lived millions of years ago. Scientists call them "living fossils."

Some of today's redwoods are thousands of years old.

Millions of years ago, during the age of the dinosaurs, Earth was warm and moist. These conditions were good for redwood trees. Redwoods grew over much of the planet. Earth's climate has changed many times since then. One million years ago, huge sheets of ice and **glaciers** covered much of the planet. Today, most of the glaciers have melted. Dinosaurs have long been extinct. But the redwood forest still grows in California.

There are many reasons for coast redwoods' survival. One reason is their bark. Redwood bark is up to 12 inches (30 cm) thick. This thick bark absorbs moisture and **insulates** the tree's core.

Redwood bark is thick and strong.

That helps protect the tree's core from burning in forest fires. The bark also contains high levels of tannin. This natural material fights off diseases and prevents insect damage.

In addition, coast redwoods are among the fastest-growing trees on Earth. They add 3 to 10 feet (0.9 to 3.0 m) in height

ANOTHER GIANT IN THE FAMILY

The coast redwood is the world's tallest tree. But a different California tree is larger. The giant sequoia grows in the Sierra Nevada. Sequoias and coast redwoods are closely related. Sequoias are tall, but they are still shorter than coast redwoods. However, the largest sequoias have much wider trunks. They contain more wood, so they are the bigger trees.

Northern California has proven to be the ideal home for coast redwoods.

each year. Redwoods can also develop new sprouts from old trees or stumps. In this way, the tree keeps on living by growing new stems from old roots. These trees cannot live where conditions are too hot or dry. But they have survived in the California fog for many generations.

CHAPTER 3

LIFE AMONG THE REDWOODS

The redwood forest is a rich ecosystem. It is filled with many plants and animals. Some are rare or **endangered** species. Keeping the forest healthy will help these species survive.

In addition to redwoods, other trees also grow in the redwood forest. Shrubs, vines, and ferns grow in the forest, too.

Many plant and animal species live among the redwood trees.

Ferns are a common sight at the base of redwood trees.

So do herbs and grasses. And that's just on the forest floor.

Above the ground level, more plants grow. Some live on the redwood trees themselves. They take root in dirt that collects on trunks and branches. The soil on redwood branches can be up to 6.5 feet (2.0 m) deep. Ferns and mosses grow in this soil. Bigger plants live in the treetops as well. Berry bushes and even small trees grow on the redwoods.

Thousands of animals live in the redwood forest. Many are mammals. Among them are black bears, foxes, and bobcats. Deer, squirrels, mice, and bats also live here. Some of these animals make their homes on or under the ground. Others live in the trees.

The forests also include flocks of birds. Sparrows, blackbirds, and others fly in the forest. Owls hunt and hoot.

Woodpeckers peck, and hummingbirds hum. The marbled murrelet is a rare seabird that spends most of its life at sea. But it makes its nest in the redwood forest. The marbled murrelet is one of the endangered species that depend on redwoods.

Reptiles and amphibians also live among the redwoods. Amphibians seek out cool, moist places. Frogs and toads gather near forest streams. Salamanders are found in wet areas. Reptiles such as snakes and lizards crawl among the trees and clearings.

In addition, the redwood forest is home to thousands of insect species. Some live

A deer roams among giant redwood trees.

on the forest floor, under leaves. Others live on the trees. Still others live in the bark. All of these plants and animals make up the forest's web of life.

GETTING WATER TO THE TOP

Similar to other trees, redwoods receive water from rain. The trees' roots collect water from the ground. But the entire tree needs water. And a redwood's top can be more than 300 feet (91 m) from its roots.

The tree works like a paper towel, sucking liquid up. Water flows in an unbroken stream through tubes within the wood. Water tends to stick together. As one bit of water goes up, it pulls the water behind it farther up the tree. Water evaporates from the tree's needles. As it does, more water moves up to replace it.

Redwood trees can be as tall as a football field is long.

CHAPTER 4

THE FUTURE OF THE FOREST

In 1850, the **old-growth** redwood forest covered 2 million acres (809,400 hectares). That's an area three times the size of Rhode Island. For thousands of years, American Indian tribes such as the Chilula and Yurok coexisted peacefully with the redwoods.

Humans and redwoods thrived together for a long time.

Things changed after white settlers discovered gold in California. Beginning in the 1850s, waves of settlers headed west. They were looking for riches. But they also built towns. So settlers chopped down thousands of redwoods to use in building their towns.

Before long, the old-growth forest started disappearing. People began working to save the ancient trees. In 1902, California created the first park to protect redwoods. While logging companies kept cutting, people continued working to save the trees. In 1968, the US Congress created Redwood National Park.

REDWOOD FORESTS

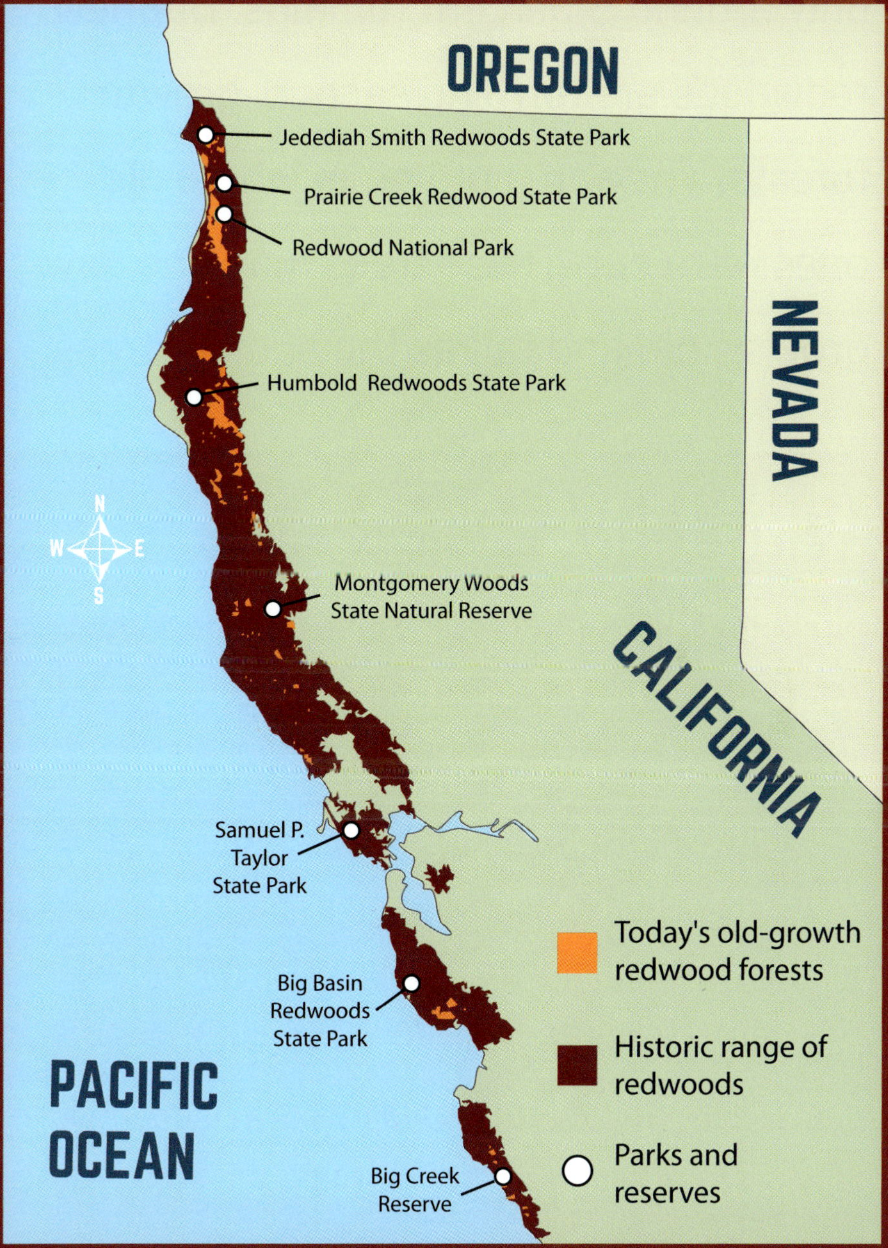

Of the old-growth redwood forest, only around 5 percent remains. But new redwoods are forming second-growth forests. They are coming in where old ones were cut. These trees may one day grow as old and tall as the ancient trees.

SAVING LUNA

In 1997, Julia Hill wanted to save an ancient redwood. She called this tree Luna. However, a lumber company planned to cut Luna down. Hill climbed onto a platform high in Luna's branches. She refused to come down. She said she would stay until the company promised to preserve Luna. For more than two years, Hill lived in the tree. Volunteers brought her food. Finally, the company agreed not to cut Luna. The tree still stands today.

Redwood trees are one of Earth's great wonders.

This is good news. Many people visit California to enjoy the redwoods. Visitors to the parks can hike and camp beneath towering trees. They look up in wonder at California's amazing redwood forest.

FOCUS ON

CALIFORNIA'S REDWOOD FOREST

Write your answers on a separate piece of paper.

1. Write a sentence that describes the main ideas of Chapter 3.

2. Would you like to visit California's redwood forest? Why or why not?

3. What caused California's redwood forest to begin shrinking in the 1850s?

- **A.** Giant forest fires burned down many of the redwood trees.
- **B.** American Indians chopped down trees for homes and canoes.
- **C.** Settlers cut down many redwood trees.

4. Redwood fossils have been found around the world. What do these fossils tell us?

- **A.** Long ago, the planet's climates were different.
- **B.** Long ago, redwood trees were stronger.
- **C.** Long ago, dinosaurs destroyed most redwoods.

Answer key on page 32.

GLOSSARY

ecosystem
The collection of living things in a natural area.

endangered
In danger of dying out.

evergreens
Plants that keep their leaves or needles all year long.

fossils
Parts of an animal or plant that remain preserved in rock.

glaciers
Large, slow-moving bodies of ice.

insulates
Protects by preventing heat from getting in or out.

old-growth
An area of a forest that has developed over many years without being disturbed.

species
A group of animals or plants that are similar.

temperate rainforest
A forest that receives large amounts of rain, in an area with cool summers and year-round temperatures usually above freezing.

TO LEARN MORE

BOOKS

Hinman, Bonnie. *Keystone Species That Live in Forests.* Hockessin, DE: Mitchell Lane Publishers, 2016.

Jackson, Donna M. *Extreme Scientists: Exploring Nature's Mysteries from Perilous Places.* Boston: Houghton Mifflin Harcourt, 2014.

Tornio, Stacy, and Ken Keffer. *Ranger Rick: National Parks!* Lanham, MD: Muddy Boots, 2016.

NOTE TO EDUCATORS

Visit **www.focusreaders.com** to find lesson plans, activities, links, and other resources related to this title.

INDEX

Answer Key: 1. Answers will vary; **2.** Answers will vary; **3.** C; **4.** A